The Hidden Treasure

Don't miss any of Bella
and Glimmer's adventures!

Unicorn Magic

Unicorn Magic

- BOOK 4 -

The Hidden Treasure

BY JESSICA BURKHART

Illustrated by Victoria Ying

Aladdin

NEW YORK   LONDON   TORONTO   SYDNEY   NEW DELHI

To Lex and Grace Carson.
You both fill my life with such love and beauty! <3

ALADDIN
An imprint of Simon & Schuster Children's Publishing Division
1230 Avenue of the Americas, New York, NY 10020
This Aladdin paperback edition March 2015
Text copyright © 2015 by Jessica Burkhart
Cover illustrations copyright © 2015 by Victoria Ying
Interior illustrations by Victoria Ying
All rights reserved, including the right of reproduction in whole or in part in any form.
ALADDIN is a trademark of Simon & Schuster, Inc., and related logo
is a registered trademark of Simon & Schuster, Inc.
Also available in an Aladdin hardcover edition.
For information about special discounts for bulk purchases, please contact
Simon & Schuster Special Sales at 1-866-506-1949
or business@simonandschuster.com.
The Simon & Schuster Speakers Bureau can bring authors to your live event.
For more information or to book an event contact the
Simon & Schuster Speakers Bureau at 1-866-248-3049 or
visit our website at www.simonspeakers.com.
Cover designed by Jessica Handelman
Interior designed by Mike Rosamilia
The text of this book was set in Arno Pro.
Manufactured in the United States of America 0315 OFF
2 4 6 8 10 9 7 5 3
Library of Congress Control Number 2014958803
ISBN 978-1-4814-1108-0 (hc)
ISBN 978-1-4424-9829-7 (pbk)
ISBN 978-1-4424-9831-0 (eBook)

Contents

1

Party Crasher

Princess Bella stared at her evil aunt, Queen Fire, trying to look brave. Bella had been having a great time with the rest of her classmates at a fun dance that her parents, King Phillip and Queen Katherine, had planned to celebrate the end of the year. But Queen Fire had been a not-so-fun party surprise.

"How long does this"—Bella pointed to the black powder that hid them both from the other guests—"last?"

"Dear niece, don't worry about our privacy," Queen Fire said in a sugar-sweet tone. Bella's aunt had raven-black hair that hung down her back, glittering eyes, and matching ruby-red lips and nails.

"Did you have to come during my party?" Bella asked.

"I can come and go whenever I please," Queen Fire said. She glanced away from Bella, taking in the happy chatter and fun as Bella's classmates danced nearby.

Bella started to say something, but she bit her lip to keep quiet. Had she imagined the flicker of sadness on Queen Fire's face?

"Please let me go," Bella begged. "Today and tomorrow are the last days I can spend with my cousin before she goes home. I know I owe you a favor, though, and I am not going back on my promise."

Images flashed through Bella's mind—picture after picture of that horrible time when Glimmer, Bella's unicorn, had run away to the Dark Forest. Bella and Glimmer had just started to get to know each other after the two had been matched on Bella's eighth birthday. But Glimmer had run away, and when Bella had found her in the scary Dark Forest, they were suddenly in the path of Queen Fire's dangerous unicorns. Bella and Glimmer had been seconds away from serious trouble before Queen Fire saved them. In turn, Bella had pledged to help her aunt if she ever needed it. And if she did not help Queen Fire, her aunt was going to take Glimmer away.

Queen Fire crossed her arms. "I had a feeling you would back out of our deal."

"I'm not letting you have Glimmer!" Bella said.

"Then I suggest you listen very carefully. There is a crystal hidden in your castle. It has, let's say, *sentimental* value to me."

"Where is it?"

Queen Fire laughed. "Niece, if I knew the answer, I would have told you. I'm not *that* evil."

"So that's what I have to do?" Bella asked. "I have to find this crystal?" She paused. "Is it hidden away for a reason? Am I going to get in trouble for finding the crystal and giving it to you?"

Queen Fire leaned close to Bella. "If you're worried about getting in trouble, then don't get caught."

Bella felt like she was underwater—like someone had stuffed cotton balls in her ears. The class party felt very far away, and she did not know what to say to her aunt.

Bella swallowed. "Is that all? Because I really need to get back and—"

"Fine." Queen Fire sighed, waving a pale hand in the air. "Go back to your party, dear. I'm getting rather tired of hiding, though. I want you at *my* castle tomorrow. We need to talk. I need to make sure you understand the importance of your task."

Bella chewed on the inside of her cheek. She

didn't want to ask more questions to keep the queen here longer, but . . .

"Can I come on Sunday? Please?"

Queen Fire stared, unblinking, at Bella. "Sunday. Before sunset, or I'll have my guards begin to ready a stall at my stables for Glimmer."

"Not a cha—"

Queen Fire vanished before Bella could finish her sentence. Bella looked down, and all the black powder had disappeared too.

Okay, pull yourself together, Bella. You can't let anyone see that you're upset.

She glanced down at her shaking hands. She walked over to a crystal punch bowl floating in the air.

"One cup, please," she said, testing out her voice. She thought she sounded like her usual self.

A ladle dipped into the bowl, filling a cup with red punch. The cup lowered itself in front of Bella.

"Thank you." Bella took the cup and sipped, trying to shake off Queen Fire's visit. She smoothed her sparkly teal dress with her free hand.

"Bella?" A familiar voice called her name.

"Over here," Bella said as she forced a smile onto her face.

Her best friends, Ivy and Clara, along with her cousin, Violet, surrounded her.

"Did you help that lady who was looking for you?" Ivy asked.

Bella nodded, grabbing Ivy's hand and tugging her forward. "Yes. Let's go back to the party."

The princess accompanied her friends and her cousin out of the tent and made a silent vow to never let Queen Fire that close to her friends ever again.

2

Swimming in Secrets

"I can't believe it's your last day here!" Bella said, sticking out her bottom lip.

"I know," Violet replied as she twirled the ends of her red hair, which was in two braids. "I begged my parents to let me stay longer, but they said I had to come home for school."

Both princesses frowned. They were each lying on a giant raft—Bella's pink and Violet's frosty white. The rafts hovered above the pool water as the girls soaked up some sun. Bella pushed the down button, and her raft lowered until it touched the water. It was a very warm day in Crystal Kingdom, and Bella was ready for a swim in one of the royal pools. Violet, Princess of Foris Kingdom, was Bella's cousin. She was a little younger than Bella.

"I can't wait till Ivy and Clara get here," Violet said, slipping off her raft and into the crystal-clear pool water. The bottom and sides of the pool were covered in clear pea-size crystals that made the water look sparkly. "I feel like I've known them forever—not less than a week!"

"They are such good friends like that," Bella agreed.

Violet climbed up the pool stairs, walked the length of the pool, and stopped in front of the diving board.

"Higher, please," Violet commanded. The white board lifted off the ground and rose a few inches into the air.

"Go, Vi!" Bella cheered.

"Cannnnnonnnnbaaaallll!" Violet yelled as

she jumped off the board, wrapping her arms around her legs.

Bella giggled as her cousin caused waves in the pool and splashed her.

Queen Katherine had spelled the pool to be just deep enough for cannonballs, but no diving was allowed. They were only allowed to jump off of it or do cannonballs when someone else was in or around the pool.

For the few seconds that Violet was underwater, Bella let out a giant sigh that she felt she had been holding inside since Queen Fire had talked to her.

Keeping secrets is so hard, Bella thought. *Where do I even begin to look for the crystal?*

There was zero chance she would tell her mom and dad, but as Bella watched Violet break the surface of the water, grinning, Bella *knew*. She had to tell her friends and her cousin. If she didn't, it would go against their rules of BFFs. Queen Katherine appeared with a basket of flowers resting in the crook of her arm. She waved at Bella, and Bella's stomach felt all flip-floppy when she waved back at the queen.

"Awesome cannonball!" Queen Katherine called out.

Violet smiled. "Thanks!" she said as she crooked her finger at her raft and it sailed through the air, stopping inches before her.

Bella rolled off her raft and slipped underwater. As she sank down a few inches, the princess rubbed her temples. She had almost fallen asleep twice on her pool float because she had been up most of the night trying to figure out every spot the crystal could be hidden. As Bella had mapped late into the night, she got more and more nervous, because she wasn't just retrieving a crystal for Queen Fire—the princess was *stealing*. Queen Fire hadn't said a word about "borrowing," so Bella didn't think Crystal

Castle would be getting the magical sparkler back. She felt like a unicorn was sitting on her chest.

Bella surfaced, swimming toward the ladder. She walked up to the diving board.

"Let me set the height," Violet said. "Okay, Bella? Or are you scared?"

Bella stuck out her tongue at her cousin. "Raise the board as high as you want!"

Violet lifted a hand out of the water. "Up, please."

The board rose and rose and *rose.*

Was Vi ever going to tell the board to stop? Bella wondered, feeling like there were teensy butterflies in her stomach.

"Please stop!" Violet called out. "That's perfect."

Silvery shimmery stairs—which glittered in the sunlight—appeared. Without thinking, Bella grasped the cool bars of the ladder and climbed to the top. The princess was afraid that if she stopped, she might back out.

"Okay! I'm doing it!" Bella said. "Here I gooo!" She ran a few steps forward, then pushed off of the board with the tips of her toes. She hugged her knees to her chest and hit the water.

She kicked to the surface and blinked through the water in her eyes. "I dare you," she said, looking at Violet. "Let me raise the board."

"Up, please," Bella said as her cousin climbed out of the pool and headed for the diving board. "Stop."

The board halted—hovering close to the area where Bella had jumped.

Violet's steps slowed as she neared the board's stairs.

"Ooh, that's pretty high," Bella called, grinning.

"Stop it!" Violet said. "You can't scare me." She climbed the stairs.

Bella raised her hands in the air. "I wasn't trying to. I was just telling the truth—you set the diving board *pretty* high." Bella kicked her feet, splashing, as she swam to her raft and climbed on top.

The princess's cousin frowned, taking a step back from the end of the board.

"I guess I could lower it," Vi muttered to herself. She shook her head. "No! Cannonball!"

Violet reached the end of the diving board in two steps. She pushed off the high dive, bringing her knees to her chest and wrapping her arms around them. Then all Bella could see was a pink blur of Vi's swimsuit and two red braids sticking up in the air just before Violet crashed into the pool, sending water everywhere.

Bella laughed. Her raft bobbed a little from the small waves that rippled across the water after Vi jumped in. Violet popped up and raised a fist in the air.

"Yes!" Violet said, grinning. "I'm the all-star champion of Crystal Castle cannonballs. I think I deserve a ribbon or, no, a *trophy*."

"Ha, ha," Bella said, sliding off her raft and into the water. "You must be joking. I have held the all-time record for the most awesome cannonballs in any of the four sky islands!"

Violet scrambled atop her raft. "Prove it."

"Who's proving what?" a voice called out.

"Yeah! Spill, because I want to play!"

Ivy and Clara, both in their swimsuits, waved from the entrance by the pool. A wide-brimmed floppy hat shielded Clara's eyes from the sun. Clara's long, strawberry-blond-colored hair was up in a pretty ponytail. Ivy's chin-length blond hair had rainbow clips holding her hair away from her face.

"Yay, we're all together!" Bella cheered.

"Get in!" Violet said, motioning toward the water. "We're trying to decide who can do a better cannonball."

"That's easy," Ivy said. "I can." Smiling, she kicked off her flip-flops and ran toward the water.

"Cannonball!" She hit the water and it sprayed everywhere. All of the girls burst into laughter.

After each girl showed off her cannonball skills, they kept on playing and swimming in the water until their fingers and toes were all shriveled up. They all shook out their beach towels and sat by the pool, waiting to dry off.

Bella rolled onto her stomach, propping her chin up on her hands. "There is something that I need to tell you guys."

The other three girls all looked at Bella.

"But you can't get too worried, okay?" Bella asked. "Promise?"

Ivy shifted her eyes to meet Clara's. Violet stared at Bella as if she was trying to determine what Bella was going to say before she said it.

"Promise," Violet finally said.

"Guys?" Bella asked, looking at Ivy and Clara.

"Promise," they said in unison.

Bella took a deep breath. "Queen Fire kind of showed up at our party yesterday."

3

A Super-Secret Mission

"What?!" Ivy, Clara, and Violet chorused.

"Queen Fire?" Ivy said. "When was she at the party? And why?"

"Why did you wait until now to tell us?" Clara asked. She sat up and crossed her arms.

"Because of this!" Bella said. "I knew you guys would be upset, and can you try to keep it down a little? I don't want my parents or anyone else to walk by and hear this."

"We have to tell Uncle Phillip and Aunt Katherine right now," Violet insisted. "You can't keep this a secret, Bella."

"Vi, please at least listen to what I have to say, okay? I didn't have to tell you guys, but I did. I told you because I know you'll all be able to help me."

Violet, Clara, and Ivy were silent.

"Okay," Clara said as Ivy and Violet nodded.

"Thank you," Bella said, sitting up on her beach towel. "Ivy, you actually met Queen Fire."

"I did? When?" Ivy asked, her mouth hanging open in surprise.

"Do you remember when you came and got me during the party? There was a woman in the food tent who wanted to see me."

"Oh, yes!" Ivy said, nodding.

"That was Queen Fire," Bella said.

She glanced around and listened. But she didn't see anyone, and all she heard was an occasional unicorn hoofbeat as they went around for a walk. Bella was also on the lookout for any Busy Bees. Busy Bees lived in Crystal Kingdom and had a *super*-annoying habit. They were very nosy! The bees searched for gossip and talk around the town and the castle. Once a Busy Bee had locked in on gossip, it would release its stinger. The stinger recorded the gossip for as long as the bee could fly near the gossiper without getting caught. Once the bee had finished, it would fly into one of the Busy Bee Boxes that were

scattered throughout the kingdom. The bee would share the gossip with other bees and would sometimes—if asked nicely—share random gossip to someone collecting honey from the box.

"Once we were alone, she dropped her disguise," the princess continued. "She wanted me to help her out and make sure I paid her back for her help."

"What do you mean?" Violet asked.

"Queen Fire saved Glimmer and Bella when they were lost in the Dark Forest," Ivy said. "As thanks, Bella promised to help Queen Fire."

"If Bella doesn't keep her promise . . ." Clara let her sentence trail off.

"If I don't keep my promise," Bella picked up, her voice wobbly, "Queen Fire will take Glimmer away for good." The princess's shoulders slumped and she sniffed, wiping her eyes with the back of her hand.

Violet gasped. "Bella! Now we *really* have to tell your parents!"

Bella shook her head. "No way. I'm not telling them, Vi. I'm trusting all of you because you're my best friends."

"What do you think she wants?" Ivy asked.

"She wants a crystal that's hidden inside the castle. I'll give her whatever she wants. Not even the biggest crystal in the world means more than Glimmer."

The other girls were quiet.

"I would do the same thing," Clara declared. Bella shot her friend a grateful smile.

"How can we help?" Clara asked.

"I'm with Clara," Ivy said. "I don't like it, but I'm in. What does the crystal do, anyway?"

"I don't know," Bella said. "I'm sure I'll find out tomorrow."

Bella, Ivy, and Clara looked at the Princess of Foris Kingdom. Violet was staring down at her toes, which were painted a cheerful yellow. Except no one was in a cheerful mood anymore.

"I *have* to leave tomorrow," Violet said. "But that doesn't mean I can't or don't want to help. Count me in."

"Thank you so much," Bella said. "There has never been anything more important to me than Glimmer. So I have to do whatever Queen Fire says. No matter what."

"I say that we don't waste another second," Violet said. "We may not have all the details, but we *do* know that Bella has to find this crystal somewhere within the castle, right?"

Bella and the other girls nodded.

"I say we start making lists and a map of places to check. I don't think we should leave out a single room," Violet added.

"Great idea!" Bella said.

"Let's get some Secret Scribble notebooks," Clara said. "I nominate Vi to draw the map. It will take a lot of work, so maybe you can finish them on the train tomorrow and send it to us with your Chat Crystal?"

Secret Scribble notebooks were the *best*. They only revealed the page's contents to the first person to open the notebook. The pages appeared blank to everyone else unless the owner wrote names in the notebook of other people who could see the pages.

"Of course, yes," Violet said. "But it's Bella's home. Don't you think . . . *oh*, right." The Foris princess grinned, and her smile seemed contagious to everyone except Bella.

"Why are you all smiling?" Bella asked. "Vi, what did that 'oh, right' mean?"

"Um, well," Violet started. "Bells, I'm sorry. I love you, but your drawing skills . . . let's just say that Clara asked the right person for this particular job."

"Hey!" Bella said. She sat up and reached for an outdoor pillow on the nearest lounge chair. She lightly tossed it at Violet, then picked up another and tossed it at Clara.

Ivy cracked up.

Bella smiled. At least they could laugh about the whole secret, scary mission! The news about Queen Fire hadn't exactly been the kind of news that the princess liked to share with her friends. It made her sad when she made *them* upset.

"Oh, so you agree with them?" Bella asked Ivy, trying to keep a fake frown on her face. "Then you can have a pillow too!"

"Nooo!" Ivy managed to say as she continued to giggle.

But there wasn't another pillow in Bella's reach. She darted to the next lounge chair and grabbed a pillow from there.

Bella launched the pillow into the air as the other girls shrieked and jumped. As they giggled and jumped into the pool, Bella was happy that she wasn't in this alone.

4

Unicorn Sparks

"That's an hour!" Ivy said, reaching over to shut off the timer. She, Bella, and Clara were on the princess's bed with vocab flash cards spread all around them.

Earlier that morning, Bella had come home from the Rainbow Rail Express Station, where she and her parents had dropped off Violet. The cousins had shared a fierce hug, and Violet had whispered that Bella had to keep her updated about Queen Fire. After Bella and her parents got back, Clara and Ivy came over to study and start on Operation: Find the Crystal.

"I'm so glad your parents let us come over," Clara said. "Studying for an hour wasn't too bad."

Queen Katherine had allowed Bella to have friends come over today only if they studied for the upcoming week's vocabulary quiz.

"An *hour* was okay," Bella said. "But being stuck in school starting tomorrow is going to take up lots of time. Time that we could be using to search for the crystal."

"I know," Ivy said. "But if we don't get good grades, then you know our parents will only let us see each other in class. And then we would really be in a big pickle!"

Bella nodded, putting a rubber band around the flash cards. "That *is* true," she agreed. "This is so the wrong week for us to be kept apart!" She leaned close to her friends. "I want to make a list of places to search for the crystal, but let me see where my parents are. Did you guys bring your notebooks?"

Ivy and Clara nodded, and each girl reached for her backpack.

Bella hopped off her bed and pressed the button next to her intercom. Long before she had even been born, cameras had been put in all over the castle and its grounds. They helped keep everyone safe.

"Where are Mom and Dad?" Bella asked, letting go of the blue button. Immediately, two screens appeared on the wall. Queen Katherine was in the living room, smiling and laughing with two of her own best friends. "Mom: check," Bella said in a whisper. King Phillip, seated at his giant desk, rubbed his chin and frowned at whatever was on the papers in front of him. "Dad: check."

"Clear?" Ivy asked.

Nodding, Bella turned off the cameras and climbed back onto her bed. "We don't have to whisper—just keep our ears open. Mom's got friends downstairs, and Dad's in the opposite wing in his office."

The princess picked up a pen she'd been using and grabbed her Secret Scribble notebook from her nightstand.

"Let me see if Violet can hang with us," Bella said, picking up her Chat Crystal. "She should be home by now." Bella put the clear, smooth stone on her palm. "Chat Crystal, please ask Violet if she can talk to me and my friends. She has to be alone."

The crystal swirled pink, purple, and yellow while it relayed Bella's message to her cousin. Within a few seconds, a light began to project up from the stone.

"Yay, she's free!" Bella said. She put the Chat Crystal on a pillow at the front of her bed. The light switched to a fuzzy outline of a person, and then Violet popped into view. Just like Bella, Ivy, and

Clara, Violet sat on her bed with her pink Secret Scribble notebook on her lap.

"Hi!" Violet said, waving. Her bright-yellow comforter covered in white daisies matched her bubbly personality.

"Hi!" Bella and her friends chorused back.

"You messaged me at the perfect time," Violet said. "I got home a few hours ago, and my parents are out at some kind of grown-up event."

"I miss you already," Bella said. "But I'm glad you're 'here' to help."

Violet stuck out her lower lip. "I miss all of you, too! I'm sorry I can't be there, Bells, but I'll do everything I can from here. Oh!" Vi held up a folded piece of paper. "This is the map I promised to draw. Hold on a second."

Violet put down the paper and placed her Chat Crystal on top. "Please send this to Princess Bella of Crystal Kingdom," she said.

The Foris princess had no sooner finished her sentence when a paper floated down from the ceiling and landed in Bella's lap.

"Got it," Bella said, smiling and holding it up so Violet could see.

"I hope it's helpful," Vi said. "I did the best I could."

"I'm sure it will be," Bella said as she unfolded the paper. "Violet!" she exclaimed.

The map was easily four times as big as Bella's notebook. Violet had managed to draw all of the sparkly and important details of the Crystal Castle. She even included the lush and beautiful gardens that were on the grounds of the castle—some of Bella's favorite places!

"Um, *wow*," Clara said.

Ivy's eyes were wide. "How did you do this?! This is amazing!"

Violet's cheeks blushed almost as red as her

hair. "Thank you! I started to draw the castle but realized that I didn't know *every* room, even though I've visited a lot."

"I live here, and *I* don't even know every room!" Bella said. All of the girls laughed.

"I virtually visited Foris Kingdom's library, and because I'm a princess, I was able to see really old maps of the castle," Violet said. "It was the perfect thing to do on the train. So I used those to help me. That map *should* have every single room of Crystal Castle on it."

"Every one is labeled," Bella said, touching the headings for KITCHEN and FIRST-FLOOR GREAT ROOM.

"Violet, thank you," Bella said. "This is going to help so much. I'm holding on to this map to use next time I'm half-asleep and my mom is calling me to breakfast!"

The cousins smiled at each other. A clock chimed in Violet's room, and Bella was soon reminded of the reason that she and her friends were all gathered.

"Is it okay if we all start throwing out ideas and I'll write them down in this notebook?" Bella asked. "Tomorrow after school, we can start with the ones that seem like the best guesses and check them off as we go. Today, after we make the list, I'll go to Queen Fire's castle."

"We'll have your back," Ivy said.

"Ivy and Clara, you won't be able to cover for Bella every second while she's searching for the crystal or with Queen Fire," Violet said. "What if you covered for them, Bella? You could assign different rooms of the castle to each other. Bella, you would know the castle the best, so maybe you can search some rooms that aren't used as much after your parents go to sleep or are busy. Rooms that aren't as familiar to Ivy and Clara."

"Smart," Clara said. "Bells, maybe you could also search any rooms—like your parents' bedroom—that would be fine if you were caught in them, but not if Ivy and I were found."

"Brilliant," Bella said.

"Everyone is a million percent sure that their notebook is *totally* secret, right?" Ivy asked, worried.

"Yes," Bella said. "I kept testing mine last night to make sure. I must have opened and closed it a dozen times."

"I did the same thing," Clara said.

"Me too," Violet added.

"Okay, so on to the list," Bella said. "Basement and basement storage rooms."

"I'll check off rooms on the map once you write them down," Clara said. She made two tiny pink check marks on Violet's map. "Don't forget—we have to really check each room. Like spies. We have to move paintings, look under rugs—stuff like that. The crystal probably isn't in plain sight."

The other girls nodded.

"How about the library?" Ivy said. She wrinkled her nose. "Oops. Sorry—I meant *libraries*."

Bella wrote that into her notebook.

The four friends worked nonstop until each wing of the castle was divided up. Bella made a big wish on all the stars in Crystal Kingdom that this plan would work.

"Glimmer, I have to tell you a secret," Bella began.

Her unicorn's purple-tinged ears swiveled back and forth—something Glimmer did when she was nervous.

A couple of hours ago, the princess and her friends had finished with their list of rooms. Bella's mom still had guests, thankfully, so the queen had been a little distracted when Bella had told her that she, Ivy, and Clara were going outside to play in the gardens and stables.

Bella had just left her friends in Snapdragon Garden and had collected Glimmer from the Royal Stables.

They were in one of the many large pastures that King Phillip and Queen Katherine kept for the royal unicorns. Bella had taken Glimmer far away from the stables so no one could hear them. She hoped the Busy Bees would stay away.

"You have to trust me and not get scared," Bella said. She smoothed her cheery sky-blue sundress and took a deep breath.

Glimmer's mostly white coat dazzled in the sunlight like thousands of diamonds. Her mane and tail were purple—the color of Bella's aura.

Bella looked into Glimmer's big brown eyes. "I'm going to Queen Fire's castle."

Glimmer snorted and threw up her head.

"Shhh, it's okay," Bella said. "I promise! I owe her a favor, remember?"

Glimmer stared at Bella with scared eyes.

Bella and Glimmer were so close that their bond allowed Bella to read Glimmer's thoughts by watching the unicorn's body language. They had been together since Bella's eighth birthday, when Glimmer had been the one, out of a lineup of royal unicorns, who had matched Bella's aura. Once a royal and a unicorn were paired, they took care of each other for life.

"You want me to take you with me?" Bella asked. "I can't. There's less of a chance that Mom and Dad will notice I'm gone if you're still here."

The unicorn shook her head, and tiny sparks began to crackle all over her body. They were like tiny firecrackers that left itsy-bitsy clouds of smoke.

Bella gasped. She put a hand on Glimmer's forehead. "Oh, Glimmer, don't be so worried about me! Is that why you're . . . *sparking*?"

Glimmer bobbed her head; her purple mane flew everywhere, some hairs staying stuck up after she'd finished moving.

"Oh, poor girl," Bella said, reaching forward and fixing the bits of mane.

She threw her arms around the unicorn's neck.

She hugged Glimmer tight. The sparks slowly stopped until the final poof of smoke disappeared. "Glimmer, please don't be scared. The best thing you can do is be brave and not let Frederick or Ben see you sparking or acting nervous. Okay?"

Frederick was in charge of the royal stables. His nephew, Ben, was his apprentice. Ben and Bella were good friends. Ben had been busy brushing a unicorn when Bella had passed on the way to Glimmer's stall. Besides the need to keep everything tip-top secret, Bella wanted to keep Ben safe, too. It was bad enough that her best friends and cousin knew—and were already so deep into the plan.

Bella swept her fingers over Glimmer's cheek. "You *really* think Queen Fire might hurt me?" She paused. "I don't, sweet girl. I saw a good side of her, *and* she's my aunt. I don't think she would ever do anything like that."

Glimmer snorted, dropping her head.

"I wouldn't go if I didn't owe her," Bella said. "The sooner I pay her back, the sooner we won't ever have to think about Queen Fire again. If I get into any sort of trouble, you'll know. Stay out here," she added with a wave of her arm. "Eat some dandelions and take a nap. That way, I'll be back when you wake up."

She hugged Glimmer, then turned away. *I hope I can keep my promise,* Bella thought. She touched the Chat Crystal in her pocket, comforted by knowing Ivy and Clara had their own Crystals in hand, waiting for any signal of trouble.

"Oof," Bella exclaimed as she jerked to a halt. She twisted around and saw that Glimmer was tugging on the hem of her dress.

Bella couldn't help but laugh. "Glimmer. Please don't worry!"

The unicorn kept her teeth clamped on Bella's dress.

Bella sighed. "Glimmer, if I don't go, then there *will* be trouble. Please."

Glimmer stared at Bella with her big brown eyes and long eyelashes. Finally, she dipped her head and let go of her dress.

"Don't worry, Glimmer. I'll be back in a unicorn minute!" Bella said. She kissed Glimmer's cheek.

Bella broke into a jog as she headed toward the castle's drawbridge. The bridge was always protected by guards and their dogs. Bella slowed to a walk as she neared the guards.

"Good day, Princess Bella," a tall, thin guard greeted the princess.

"Same to you," Bella replied. She smiled at that guard and the one on her other side. He bowed his head as Bella passed.

Bella walked along the drawbridge and let out a huge sigh. The guards were behind her! That meant—

40

"Princess!"

Bella stopped in her tracks.

"Yes?" Bella said, slowly turning around. Her heart pounded in her chest and her palms sweated. *Keep your cool,* she thought. *Don't let the guards see that you're nervous!*

One of the guards walked up to her, towering over her.

Bella swallowed hard. Was her mission over before it even began?

"This fell out of your pocket," the guard said.

The guard placed a small, folded piece of notebook paper on Bella's waiting hand. She closed her fingers around the paper.

"Thank you," the princess said. "This was a recipe that I needed. I'm going to the sunray berry patch. My friends are staying here to find the other ingredients for sunray pie in my mom's gardens. I'll be back in a bit." Bella forced herself to stop rambling.

With a little wave to the guards, she was off again. Bella hurried—the longer she was gone, the higher the chance that she would get caught. She hoped her mom would be busy with friends the entire time that she was away, so that Ivy and Clara wouldn't be put to the test of covering for the missing princess.

Bella acted as if she was going to take a left and go to the sunray berry patch. She glanced behind her, and the second she was out of sight, she went in the opposite direction toward the Dark Forest. Cutting through the scary woods was the fastest way to Queen Fire's. This was definitely a trip that Bella wanted to make as fast as possible.

She slipped the paper that she'd been clutching into one of her jacket pockets. It was a very important note that she had written and then put a Go Home and Find Parents spell on. In the note, Bella told her parents that she was at Queen

Fire's castle in the Blacklands and needed help.

If anything went wrong while Bella was with Queen Fire, all she had to do was drop the paper onto the ground. It would zip through the air in millions of little pieces and turn back into a readable note only when it reached the king or queen.

A compass was in her other pocket. It would help her find the fastest path to Queen Fire's castle.

Bella stopped at the edge of the Dark Forest. She took a deep breath, trying to calm her nerves. She looked back toward Crystal Castle. The sun was high in the cloudless sky. Knee-high emerald-green grass grew on both sides of the cobblestone path she had just traveled along. Rainbow butterflies floated through the air, some stopping on pink, purple, and yellow tulips that dotted the fields.

In front of Bella was nothing but darkness.

A crow cawed, and the noise made the hairs on Bella's arms stand up. She shivered even in the warm air. The trees lining the forest entrance were leafless and skinny. The temperature dropped with each step closer to the forest—a place forbidden to Bella and all of her friends and classmates.

"You can do this," Bella said out loud. "This is for Glimmer." She inhaled, saying a silent thank-you to Ivy, Clara, and Violet. The princess had a feeling that it was going to take all of them to pull this off.

5

The Queen's Castle

The Dark Forest swallowed all of the sunlight as Bella took a few steps inside. She pulled the compass crystal from her pocket. She held it in her hand, ready to give it instructions.

"Queen Fire's castle," Bella said. Her voice was shaky—something that she had to fix before she spoke to Queen Fire. She couldn't show the queen how scared she was.

The compass shone a rainbow of light forward on the ground, pointing the way. Bella started to follow its path, then turned around. She could not see Crystal Kingdom anymore. It was as if the trees

that she had passed had grown together to trap her inside the forest. Bella took another deep breath and kept going.

Buzz!

Bella swatted the air with both of her hands. A basketball-size fly that glowed in the dark zoomed toward her. The Hairy-Scary—a fly native to the forest—had bright-yellow wings and bulging green eyes. It was covered in glowing orange fur.

The Dark Forest was full of gross bugs!

"Go away!" Bella shouted as the Hairy-Scary headed toward her. She ducked before it ran into her, then started running, not even looking at the compass.

Bella ran until she couldn't hear the fly's wings. She slowed down, looking behind her. Nothing but darkness and—"Oompf!"

The princess landed on her knees, the compass

flying from her hand and landing facedown just ahead of her.

Bella hurried to her feet even though her knees throbbed. She swiped the compass from the ground, blowing dirt off of it. The princess used the compass as a flashlight to see what had caused her fall. A thin tree root was raised just high enough to catch her foot.

"Please stay here, compass," Bella said. She removed her hand from under the compass, and it stayed in the air while she looked at her knees. Thankfully, the soft forest dirt had prevented her from getting too hurt—there was only a small cut on her left knee.

"Oh, *great!*" Bella said, pulling the compass closer. Her dress was now streaked with dirt, thanks to the fall and where she had wiped her hands, not knowing that they were so dirty.

Ivy and Clara will help me do a cleanup spell,

Bella thought. *I'll worry about Mom or Dad seeing my dress and knees when I'm home safe.*

Bella plucked the compass out of the air and found a semi-clear path. She walked for several minutes before the towering trees began to thin out and she finally saw the sky. It was no longer the brilliant blue that it had been when the princess had left home. Full black clouds rolled across the gray sky. Bella's heartbeat jumped up as fast as a hummingbird's wings because of what she spotted next. Not far in the distance, smoke billowed into the air. Two black towers with triangle-shaped tops stretched into the sky.

Queen Fire's castle.

Bella walked toward the smoke, this time keeping a closer eye on the trail.

It could have been minutes or hours when the princess stopped. Fear—and a tiny bit of curiosity—ran through her. This was it. She was glad, no matter how scared she had been, that she had come alone. She didn't think her aunt would be happy if she brought company—like Ivy or Clara—along on her first visit.

She tried to be brave, but it was hard. Who knew what was in the castle? Knowing her aunt, there could be *anything* beyond those castle doors. The red unicorn that had almost attacked Glimmer was scary enough. She patted the note in her pocket and swallowed hard. Everything would be okay as long as she had that note. Her parents could rescue her. Bella stopped when the entire castle came into view. It was as big as her own, but made of glass instead of stone. Two red unicorns stood guard on either side of the door.

This is it. I have to save Glimmer, Bella thought.

As she walked closer to the castle doors, she watched colors flickering in the glass, first red, then black, finally purple. *Purple—that's my aura,*

Bella thought. Why was that? She didn't have time to think about it, though, because almost all too soon she had reached two unicorns on concrete pedestals standing guard. They had black manes and were more muscular-looking than the royal unicorns.

"My name is Bella. *Princess* Bella. I'm here to see Queen Fire," she announced to the unicorn guards. They sidestepped away from the door, their hooves striking the concrete, as the door swung open.

Bella stepped carefully into the great hall, looking around her. The inside was glass, but without the colors swirling, like the outside. It looked like her own castle with different colors. There was a large painting at the end of the hall that caught her eye. In the painting, Queen Fire stood with her unicorns, with one on each side of her. Red and black rugs covered the floor with dizzying zigzag designs.

Not sure what to do, Bella walked into the

closest room and sat down on a red velvet couch. It faced an empty fireplace. There were no family pictures on the walls of Queen Fire's castle. For a minute, Bella actually felt sad for her mom's sister.

The princess shivered as she looked around the room. Suddenly, with a whoosh of black smoke, a fire appeared in the fireplace and warmed the room up instantly.

"You came after all, dear niece," Queen Fire said. She walked around to face Bella. Her long, black, wavy hair tumbled down her back. She wore red crystal earrings that sparkled in the firelight.

"I promised that I would come," Bella said. "I need you to keep your promise and not hurt Glimmer."

"As long as you hold up your end of the bargain, I will keep my word," Queen Fire said.

"What does this crystal do?" Bella asked. "Why do you need it?"

"That answer comes in due time," Queen Fire

said. A black leather chair shot forward. Sitting down, the queen looked over at Bella. "Do the king and queen know you're here?"

"No—"

"Oh, dear," Queen Fire said. A look of what might have been sadness flickered across her face. "You injured yourself on the journey. Are you hurt?"

"No," Bella said, shaking her head. "I'm fi—"

Before she could finish her sentence, the queen snapped her fingers. A short man in a white coat trotted into the room, stethoscope around his neck and a black bag in hand.

"Your Highness?" the man asked, looking at Queen Fire.

"Dr. Foster, please tend to my niece's injuries," Queen Fire said.

"Really, I'm okay," Bella said. "Thank you, but—"

"I'll return in a moment," Queen Fire interrupted. She disappeared, leaving Bella with the doctor.

The doctor, who had a kind face and thick glasses, placed his bag on the floor.

"I'm Dr. Foster," he said, holding out a hand.

Bella shook his hand. "I'm Bella."

"Do you mind if I take a look at your knees?" he asked. His silver hair and easy manner made Bella feel at ease.

"Okay," she said.

The doctor asked Bella how she had fallen and applied a disinfectant that stung a little. A quiet woman had come with a bowl of steaming-hot water and soap as the doctor treated Bella. She held the bowl while Bella washed dirt and grime from her hands. Then the maid sprayed something that foamed onto the dirty parts of Bella's dress. In seconds, the foam disappeared, and so did the stains. The servant left without uttering a word. Dr. Foster smoothed a small bandage over Bella's cut just as Queen Fire reappeared.

"It was lovely to meet you, Bella," Dr. Foster said. "Safe travels home."

"Thank you, doctor," Bella said, smiling at him.

He bowed to Queen Fire and disappeared.

"Are you hungry?" Queen Fire asked. She didn't wait for an answer from Bella. Two silver plates floated in the air, holding forks and a kind of cake Bella had never seen before. It was a chocolate cake topped with dark-red berries.

Bella was starving after her journey through the Dark Forest—but she was scared to eat it. *What if it's a trick?* She watched as Queen Fire took a plate and fork for herself.

"A Dark Forest specialty," the queen said. "Try it." She dug her fork into the cake.

Bella finally took a bite of the cake. She was relieved when she tasted a rich dark chocolate. She took another small bite. She sneaked a look toward her aunt. This was perfectly normal. A niece and an aunt eating dessert. Bella's mind wandered as she thought about what it would be like to have a *nice* Queen Fire in her life.

"Your castle is really . . . *interesting*," Bella said. "Um, thank you for inviting me, but I can't stay long. My friends are covering for me at home."

"The fact that this is your first visit to your aunt's castle is sad. How wrong my sister was to keep me a secret from you. It was quite a pleasure to see you on your eighth birthday. I'm not forgetting your dear friends, and unicorn, of course," Queen Fire said. Her eyes were dark as coal.

Whatever "normal" niece-and-aunt-relationship thoughts Bella had vanished.

"My mom wasn't wrong. You're *bad* and you steal unicorns."

Queen Fire smirked.

"Please just tell me anything I need to know about the crystal. The sooner I get home, the faster

I can find it." Bella rested her hands on her lap after her plate and fork floated away. She didn't want Queen Fire to see them shaking.

"Oh yes, the reason I brought you," Queen Fire said.

"The special crystal is hidden in a vault. I'm guessing that vault is inside the castle."

"Guessing?" Bella asked. "Does that mean it could be *anywhere*?" She felt a bit sick with this new piece of information. It was already enough to have an entire castle to search. But if the vault could be on the *grounds* . . .

"Not anywhere," Queen Fire said, scowling. "It's definitely in the castle, and I wouldn't waste your time looking on the grounds. The crystal is very important to me."

"Why?" Bella asked.

"It is"—the queen paused—"personal."

"I can get it for you. I mean, I can try. I'll look

everywhere for it. Once I find it in the vault, I'll bring it to you," Bella promised. *What if she wants to be part of our family again?*

Queen Fire stared blankly at her, tilting her head a little. "No, princess, you must get me into the castle. You can remove it from its hiding place, but only I can take it from Crystal Castle. The crystal will lose all of its worth to me if you try to take it off castle grounds. I'm the only one who can remove it." Queen Fire paused. "Well, so can your mother."

"Only you and Mom?" Bella asked. "Why just you two?"

The queen shot Bella a dark look that made the princess swallow and forget her next question.

"But my dad said that if you ever came to our castle again, he would throw you in jail! We would *never* make it past the guards, and—"

"Bella, remember our agreement," Queen Fire pointed out.

Bella looked at her. A vision of Glimmer's beautiful white coat turning red flashed in front of her eyes.

"I'll get you into the castle. I'll do anything!" Bella said. "But you must promise me that you won't hurt my family, me, or my unicorn."

"All those precious things will be kept safe. You have my word. Hurry home before your parents discover that you're missing. And, darling Bella? You have one week to find the crystal and get me safely inside Crystal Castle. Or Glimmer is mine."

One week?! Bella felt like she had eaten too many pieces of sunray pie. There was no way they could search the castle in just one week. But she had no choice.

"Fine. I'll do it," Bella said.

"So you shall. And to show that I'm a woman of my word, I will create a contract for us," Queen Fire said. She clapped her hands, and with a puff of black smoke, a contract appeared. Bella read the

59

words carefully and saw that Queen Fire hadn't lied. The paper said that if she helped her aunt, Glimmer was safe.

The contract hovered in the air, a dark black *X* marking the spot for Bella's name. Bella grabbed the black pen floating next to the paper. She closed her eyes for a second and then dashed off her name. The ink glowed in red and then turned to gold. The contract disappeared in the same black smoke.

"Excellent," Queen Fire said. She waved her hand. "You may go. I'll look forward to hearing about your progress each day."

Without a look at her aunt, Bella almost stumbled over her own feet as she hurried out of the room. She wanted to be home and pretend this hadn't happened.

"Bella?"

The princess jerked to a halt, slowly spinning to face Queen Fire.

"Don't forget. If you fail, Glimmer is mine."

6

Search Party

Once Bella's feet hit the dirt outside the castle, she bolted for the Dark Forest. She ran so fast that not even the speediest Busy Bee could catch up to her.

She slowed to a jog and made an abrupt U-turn when she realized that she had no berries! Oops! She hurried back to the sunray berry bushes and pulled a few handfuls into the tote that she had hidden at the edge of the berry patch.

I could have blown my cover on the first day! Bella scolded herself. She forced herself to breathe and pasted a smile on her face. She glanced down at her watch—she had been gone for a little over an hour.

The guards tipped their heads. "Greetings, Princess Bella," a different, smiling guard said. "The previous guard informed me of your trip." He tipped his head toward the berry tote. "Hard time finding good, ripe berries?"

"Oh, um, yes," Bella said. She forced herself to laugh. "I did something silly—I lay down on the grass for a minute to watch the clouds, and I fell asleep." She patted the heads of the two nearby guard dogs. She was afraid the words I AM A GIANT FIBBER would pop up with an arrow pointing to her.

But nothing happened. The dogs' wet noses didn't turn red signaling danger or sensing that someone was *very, very* nervous—nervous like they were hiding a secret or about to attempt to smuggle someone onto the castle grounds.

The guard smiled. "I'm just relieved that you're safe."

With a wave to the guards, Bella pulled out her Chat Crystal.

I'M BACK! she wrote to her friends. MEET ME IN MY ROOM? She didn't want to spend time searching the dozens of gardens for her friends.

The Chat Crystal vibrated and turned bubble-gum pink. ON OUR WAY! came from Clara's crystal. Bella put the crystal back in her pocket and looked out to the pasture where she had left Glimmer. She spotted the gorgeous unicorn and whistled to get Glimmer's attention. Glimmer's eyes connected with Bella's, and it made the princess willing to make the trek to Queen Fire's castle every day if it meant coming home to her unicorn.

Bella blew Glimmer a kiss. "I'll come see you later!" she called. Glimmer let out a loud whinny and kicked up her heels, dashing across the grass.

Once inside, Bella dumped the berries into a plastic bowl for Thomas, the main chef. He could whip up something tasty with the berries.

Heading toward her room, the princess felt a little better. The canopy bed with its soft lavender sheets and big fluffy comforter always made her smile. She looked over at the pictures with her friends and then a picture of Glimmer. The picture frames changed colors according to the sunlight. Right now the frame was a soft pink. Bella was glad it wasn't red. She didn't need a reminder of Queen Fire.

"You're safe!" Ivy said as she dashed through the doorway, startling Bella. She ran up to Bella and hugged her hard, with Clara right behind her. The friends group-hugged, and Ivy and Clara hopped onto Bella's bed. Bella typed a quick message to Violet, letting her cousin know that she was home safe and would message her later.

"Tell us everything," Clara said. "Don't leave out *one* detail!"

"What was the castle like?" Ivy asked, her big blue eyes open super wide.

"I'll tell you both everything, but first, did my mom or dad notice that I wasn't with you guys?" Bella asked.

"Queen Katherine found us once," Ivy said. "Clara and I were sitting on one of the benches in the Sunshine Garden."

"We heard someone heading toward us, so we started talking about the sunray pie we were excited to make," Clara said.

"What did my mom say?" Bella asked, feeling like her heart was beating a thousand times a minute.

"She just said that sunray pie sounded good, and before she could ask, we told her that you were out getting berries at a new patch you had found. We told her that we'd stayed behind to look through the gardens for new ingredients that we wanted to try in the pie."

"I'm sorry that you had to lie," Bella apologized. "I should have thought more about that when I asked you to cover for me."

"Ivy and I talked about that while you were gone," Clara said. "We hate lying too, but not when it's for the right reasons. Keeping Glimmer is *definitely* a right reason."

Bella launched into the story of her afternoon, not leaving out a single detail. Then she flashed a grateful smile to the girls. "You guys are the best friends in the world. You covered for me today. I wouldn't have gotten away with it without you. Now I have to start the search for the vault that has the crystal."

"What do you mean '*I* have to start'?" Ivy asked, tucking a lock of hair behind her ear.

"You and Violet have been so amazing, from maps to talking to my mom, but I can't ask you guys to do more. I know what I said before, but I changed my mind. I should do this on my own."

"Um, no, best friend," Clara said. She and Ivy glanced at each other, then looked at Bella.

"We know you so well," Ivy said. "Clara and I knew you'd say all of that stuff. But we're not going to let you change the plan we all agreed to."

Clara touched Bella's arm. "We're going to help you whether you like it or not. But it would be a lot easier if you just liked it already!"

Bella laughed, shaking her head. "You two aren't going to give up, are you?"

"Nope," Ivy said. "So get out Violet's map and let's start checking rooms off that list."

The princess was quiet for a moment as she looked at her friends. Finally she let out a giant sigh. "Okay, okay!" Bella said, smiling. "If you *insist.*"

"We do," Clara said. "I have to be home in a couple of hours, so let's go! Where should we start?"

Bella scanned the map. "How about we all start in the great room? We'll be searching for it while totally being out in the open. If someone comes into the room, just pretend we're playing a game."

"Let's go!" Ivy said, hopping off Bella's bed. "We should look on our way."

The search was on! It took the friends five times as long to get to the great room as usual. The hallways from Bella's room to the downstairs were clear. The girls spread out in the great room. Bella slid a giant photograph of herself as a baby to the left and touched the bare wall. After an hour, they found a book that Bella had been looking for, a stale cookie, and a sparkly butterfly barrette. But there was no crystal to be found. At least, not yet.

7

Tick, Tock

Bella's alarm chimed, playing the official Crystal Kingdom anthem to wake her up. She hummed along as she pushed the button on the rainbow-shaped alarm clock to turn it off. Most mornings, if she didn't wake up at the first chirp of the alarm, the clock would shine a light on her bed. The light would turn a rainbow of colors, getting brighter until she got up. Today was different.

The sun was streaming through her window and covering everything in a nice warm light. The North Tower had the best views, and her bedroom was one of her favorite places in the whole world.

She especially loved to watch the unicorns grazing in the pasture. From her window seat she could see Kiwi and Scorpio, her parents' unicorns, and Glimmer. Their soft coats shone under the sun. Everything looked like it was perfect in Crystal Kingdom.

But it isn't, Bella thought. Today was Day Four. Day Four out of the seven that Queen Fire had given her to find the vault containing the crystal. On each of the previous days, Bella, Clara, and Ivy had searched the castle, checking room after room for the vault. Queen Katherine had allowed Bella's friends to stay after school for three days in a row when Bella told her that they had a special project together. They did: finding the vault.

The girls checked in with Violet often with updates and where they had searched. This crystal was harder to find than a piece of a spelled secret note! The number of rooms checked kept going up while the amount of time left kept going down.

Thankfully, Queen Katherine and King Phillip had been busy with a new Crystal Kingdom project—a royal secret, of course. Bella didn't even care what the secret project was—she was grateful that it kept her parents busy. Poor Lyssa—the princess's handmaiden, who was like an older sister—was out with the flu. As much as Bella wanted Lyssa to be well, it made it easier for Bella and her friends to search without her at the castle.

Only today, Friday, and Saturday are left, Bella thought. She buried her head in her pillow, trying not to panic. She took a few deep breaths and remembered that she had Violet, Clara, and Ivy on her side. They would find the vault.

She picked a pretty purple dress that had a dark-purple hem. The effect looked like the edges of one of Crystal Kingdom's beautiful sunsets. It was the perfect dress for Bella, and she was happy because it was the color of her aura. She pulled on her silver shoes and admired how they sparkled.

"Bella! Breakfast," Queen Katherine said on the intercom. Bella's tummy rumbled. She remembered how Queen Fire could seem like a person and not an evil queen for a moment. The smell of pancakes came into her room, and she shook her head free of anything but the thought of her breakfast with her parents for now. Bella hurried over to the intercom and pushed the button before her mom could call again.

"Coming!"

Bella quickly yanked her comforter up to the top of her bed and fluffed her pillows. They were a little sideways and lumpy, but it would have to do.

She darted out of her bedroom and skipped downstairs, ready to fill her belly with the cook's delicious food. Her feet flew across the castle's floors as she hurried into the great dining hall.

She took her place in her favorite chair, which had a big, soft velvet cushion. As Bella sat down, one of the kitchen staff, Rebecca, came in carrying their plates.

"Fresh hot scrambled eggs and berry pancakes for the princess," she said. The cook had drawn a whipped cream smiley face on her pancakes, with berries for eyes. It looked delicious, and Bella was hungry!

"Thanks, Rebecca, this is so cute," Bella said. She took her fork and dug in.

"You keep eating pancakes like that, and you're going to turn into a pancake," King Phillip said. His green eyes twinkled to show Bella he was kidding. Bella rolled her own eyes. It was a joke he made often, but she loved it.

"Dad!" Bella laughed.

She ate everything on her plate, then glanced at the clock on the wall. She wanted to talk to Ivy and Clara before school started about where they needed to look today.

"Can I be excused?" Bella asked.

"You may," Queen Katherine said. Rebecca came over from where she was waiting and took her plate.

Bella thanked her and scooted her chair back. Before the queen could ask where she was going, she ran up the stairs, down the hall, and into her bedroom. She grabbed her book bag and went out the front door, hopping over a shrub and finding Ivy and Clara already waiting near one of the castle's many water fountains.

"What's wrong?" Bella asked Clara. Her friend was frowning, and her arms were across her chest.

"I'm so, so sorry, Bella," Clara said. "My mom told me this morning that I have to come home after school today."

"It's okay," Bella said, feeling her heart race a

little bit. "You've been here every day after school. Ivy and I—"

"I can't stay either," Ivy interrupted. "I tried *everything*, but my parents both said I had to come home this afternoon because I've been staying at your house all this week."

Bella felt panic start to well up inside her, but she didn't want her friends to see. They had been doing *nothing* but helping her, and they already felt bad.

"It's okay," Bella said. "I'm so sorry if I got you in trouble with your parents. You each have searched with me every single day. I'm not mad or upset—I promise."

Bella's promise was real. She wasn't mad the tiniest bit. She was just scared. Scared that she had to try to find the crystal herself with time running out.

"Are you sure?" Ivy asked, chewing her bottom lip.

"Completely sure," Bella said. "It will be the

perfect day for me to check some rooms that only I should be in. Come on. Let's get to class." She smiled, wanting her friends to believe that she really was okay.

But the truth was she was anything but okay.

8

Hiding in Plain Sight

Bella fake-smiled her way through the entire school day. Clara and Ivy kept asking her over and over if she was okay, and she said yes every time. For once, Bella had actually been happy when her friends left the castle to go home after school.

The second she closed the front door, the smile slipped from Bella's face. She took the stairs two at a time and threw her backpack on the floor. She bit the inside of her cheek to keep from crying.

Tears are not going to find the vault, she told herself. *You can't fall apart now. You can do this.*

Bella took a few deep breaths and closed her

eyes. All she saw was Glimmer. The unicorn's sweet face made her smile. Bella's smile widened to a grin when she thought about the stubborn patch of Glimmer's mane that was determined to have a permanent curl—no matter how much Bella combed it before finally deciding to leave it alone. It was one of the things that made Glimmer unique, and it was fitting for the sometimes stubborn unicorn!

I'll get my homework out of the way, and then the search is on, Bella thought.

She got off her bed, picked up her backpack, and sat at her desk. She pulled out her books and opened her blue assignments notebook.

"Hi, sweetie."

Bella looked up at her mom, who stood in the doorway. "Hi. You look so pretty!"

Queen Katherine looked elegant in a flowing green dress, and her long blond hair was styled into perfect waves. "Thank you, Bells. Dad and I have a special dinner tonight. Official kingdom business. I'm sorry that we're going to be out late on a school night."

"It's okay, Mom," Bella said. "I'll just be doing homework. You're not going to miss anything that interesting!"

Queen Katherine smiled. "I happen to think *everything* you do is interesting. I just feel especially bad leaving you while Lyssa is out sick again. Are you sure you don't mind? You could come to dinner if you'd like."

"I've got a lot of homework. But thanks, Mom." Bella reached her arms into the air. "Hug."

The queen laughed and walked over to Bella. Standing, the princess snuggled into her mom's arms, smelling the familiar scent of the queen's favorite perfume—Sunray Delight.

Queen Katherine let go of Bella and ran a hand

over her daughter's cheek. "You sure you're okay with your dad and me going out?"

"Positive."

"I'll come and say good night when I get home," Queen Katherine said. "Love you."

"Love you, Mom."

Bella opened her assignment notebook, determined to keep her focus on schoolwork. But her eyes strayed to the Secret Scribble notebook.

"You cannot go looking for the vault until your homework is done," Bella said aloud. "So focus."

She worked through a set of twenty math problems and read the assigned chapter in her history textbook. For English, she had to read the first chapter of the next book her class was reading—*Kingdoms from A to Z*, a collection of essays from people who lived on the four different sky islands.

Oops. Mom ordered that book for me last week,

and I forgot to ask her for it. Hopefully, it's on the bookcase in the great room.

Bella headed downstairs and scanned the books on the brown bookcase. Usually her parents put new books horizontal on the shelves until after they had read them. But the book Bella needed wasn't easy to spot.

"Is that it?" she wondered out loud, reaching upward. Maybe one of the maids had stuck the book in with the rest by mistake. The book's spine was solid black—nothing gave away the title. *Weird,* Bella thought.

Bella touched the book and it *vibrated.* She yanked back her hand as if she had been shocked. Her mouth fell open as the bookcase slid to the left. The princess looked around to see if anyone else in the house—a maid or *anyone*—was passing by and seeing what she was seeing.

Then Bella understood. She knew exactly what

the bookcase had been hiding. She, Ivy, and Clara had been searching the entire castle for the thing that had been hidden in one of the busiest spots in the castle: the vault. *Calm down,* Bella told herself. *You don't even know for sure.* But something in her went against every nagging little thought that she could be wrong. Deep, deep in her gut she knew this bookcase wasn't hiding a secret tea room. The bookcase was hiding the vault.

Bella pulled on the book again, putting the bookcase back in its usual spot. She had to message Ivy and Clara—they deserved to see the crystal when Bella did.

Bella ran up to her room, swiping her Chat Crystal off her desk.

I FOUND IT!!! she messaged to Ivy, Clara, and Violet.

Seconds later, her Chat Crystal lit up with messages.

BELLA!! WHERE?!

WHAT DOES IT LOOK LIKE??

I KNEW YOU'D FIND IT!

For the first time in four days, Bella felt like she could breathe again. She would wait for Ivy and Clara so they could see the crystal together. In this moment, though, there was only one thing on her mind: getting to Glimmer and telling her that she was safe. The vault had been found, and she had nothing to worry about.

Almost.

9

Be Our "Guest"

Princess Bella looked out at Crystal Castle from one of her favorite places: her window seat. She watched two young royal unicorns playfully nip each other, then dash off as they seemed to be playing a game of Unicorn Tag. Bella's eyes were on them, but her mind was somewhere else. She replayed the last few days in her head. Just as she had been doing long before sunup.

The day after she had accidentally discovered the vault, Bella had gone inside with Ivy and Clara. The crystal wasn't in a display case with bright lights shining on it as Bella had expected. Instead the girls had had to go through more books—dozens of them—before finding it. The smallish room had shelves from wall to wall. Every possible inch of shelf space was filled with books. A fake book had a hole cut into it, and inside rested a pearl-colored gem about half the size of Bella's fist. Bella had sent a photo of it to Queen Fire.

The queen messaged back on a job well done, and the only—and most important—step left was for Bella to sneak Queen Fire into the castle to get it.

Now goose bumps suddenly dotted Bella's arms, even in the warm air. Today was The Day. The day that Queen Fire was coming for the crystal. Bella had waited and waited for the right opportunity over the past couple of days, but there hadn't been a good time to sneak Queen Fire onto the castle grounds. It had been driving Bella crazy that she was *so* close to keeping Glimmer safe, but she had to keep waiting. But no more.

If I don't do it today, she thought, *I lose Glimmer. Forever.*

Bella sat up straight, squared her shoulders, and took a deep breath. *No one* was taking her unicorn. Not after everything she had done to try to keep Glimmer safe.

It's not like Queen Fire is a beginner at all of this spying and hiding stuff, Bella reminded herself. *She is an evil queen. She doesn't want to get caught.*

Bella looked at the drawbridge, which was guarded like usual with someone on each side. Not as though she had planned to meet Queen Fire and walk—

"Bella?"

The princess jumped at her mom's voice.

"Oh, honey! I'm sorry that I scared you," Queen Katherine said from Bella's doorway. She walked over and put her arms around her daughter. "Is everything all right? You've been jumpy lately."

Bella *hated* that she was about to lie to her mom.

"I'm fine, Mom!" Bella declared. "Promise! I think it's all of the clarity berries I've been having at breakfast. They give me so much energy that I'm all squirmy until bedtime."

The queen laughed.

Part of what Bella said *was* true. Clarity berries, named after how they looked, were clear square berries. The princess *had* been eating more of them than usual.

Queen Katherine squeezed Bella's hand. "Okay. Sweetie, I'm sorry that your dad and I have been so busy lately. This is the last weekend that we'll be in and out—I promise."

Bella squeezed her mom's hand back. It was the only time *ever* that she hadn't been sad that her parents were very busy.

"It's okay, Mom," Bella said. "I'm fine. Promise."

In a couple of hours, Bella hoped that what she had just told her mother would actually be true.

"C'mon, please, c'mon!" Bella murmured under her breath.

If someone had told Bella that she would soon be standing in her great room, wishing for Queen Fire to hurry up and appear beside her, Bella would have laughed hysterically. But that was exactly what she was doing.

Ivy and Clara had split up—Ivy trailing Queen Katherine and Clara keeping an eye on King Phillip. Their jobs were to come and give Bella a heads-up if either one of her parents were headed into the castle. Moments earlier, Ivy had messaged via Chat Crystal that Queen Katherine was busy gardening, and Clara had sent word that King Phillip was inspecting the royal stables.

If only Queen Fire would get here already, take

her crystal, and go! *What if her new spell isn't working?* Bella thought. She crossed her fingers that she was wrong.

Over the past few days, Queen Fire had been working out the best way to enter the castle's property. The queen had messaged Bella that she had also been working on her disappearing-into-smoke act, trying to keep the noise and smoke to a minimum.

"I like what my sister has done with this room."

Bella jumped, clapping her hands over her mouth as she almost screamed. She whirled around.

"You scared me!" Bella said to Queen Fire. "I was starting to worry that you couldn't find a way to access the castle."

"I had to finish my tea first, Bella."

Bella tilted her head, forcing back her annoyance. It didn't matter. Nothing else mattered but the crystal. "This way," she said.

Bella faced the bookcase that led to the small room. She still couldn't believe that the vault's hidden door was nothing more than a bookcase in the great room. All of the time that she and her friends had been searching, the vault had been hiding in plain sight after all.

Bella had to press on the spine of one "book" that looked no different from the rest. But it was quite different. She slid a finger along the spine and *bzzzz!* The book vibrated ever so slightly. The bookcase slid to the side, allowing a space just wide enough for a person to enter. Bella was grateful for the button. It allowed her, Ivy, and Clara easy vault access.

"Okay, we're in," Bella said in a whisper, turning to her aunt. "And I think . . ."

Bella let her sentence trail off. The queen wasn't behind her. Her aunt stood near the end of one of the cream-colored love seats near the fireplace. She had a large, silver-framed photo in one hand

and swiped at her cheek with the other. Her nails weren't painted bloodred.

I can't believe I missed that, Bella thought. She had been maybe a teensy bit preoccupied with, oh, making sure her parents were gone, worrying about the guards, hoping the dogs wouldn't pick up her aunt's scent. . . .

Bella left the hidden door and quietly walked up to her aunt.

"You were so tiny then," Queen Fire said. She ran her finger across the glass, stopping near a toothless, smiling baby Bella, who was in a bouncy chair in a pink ruffly outfit. "I bet you didn't know that pink is actually my favorite color."

Before Bella could respond, Queen Fire put back the photo, slid past her, and entered the vault. Bella quickly pressed the button to slide the bookcase back into place. Lights flickered as soon as they stepped inside.

"This is it," Bella said with a wave of her hand. The smallish room had shelves from wall to wall. Every possible inch of shelf space was filled with books—a lot of them, Mom and Dad had pointed out, were from their school days. The rest? She looked up at the white shelves that towered over her head. Bella just *knew* those books would be hers someday. Fun things like how to dress like a queen, the master interior design book of the castle, and a list of every royal unicorn that had been at Crystal Castle.

"So it was in a book right here," Bella said. She reached for the book, frowning. It was heavier than she remembered. She opened the book to find, well, a book. Pages. Lots and lots of pages.

"What's wrong?" Queen Fire asked.

Bella put the book on a table behind her. "Nothing. I'm sorry—I grabbed the wrong book. It's this one."

She grabbed another book off the shelf and

flipped it open. There was no cutout box. No sparkling crystal. Just words.

"All right, what's going on?" Queen Fire asked. "If this is some sort of trick to lure me to the castle . . ."

"It's not a trick!" Bella said, pleading with her aunt. "I promise, the book was right here! I opened it and saw the crystal. I'm not lying."

She yanked another book off the shelf. And another.

"I'm guessing that this is your first experience with a book shuffle spell," Queen Fire said.

"A what?" Bella asked.

Queen Fire sighed. "It's a kind of protection magic. You found the correct book, and to make it a little harder, the books reordered themselves when you left."

"Oh no," Bella said. "We have to start all over again."

Queen Fire moved toward a shelf and plucked

off a book. She opened it, then set it on the floor.

"One down," she said.

"We have to move faster than that," Bella said. "I mean, I don't think anyone is going to come in here, but I can't stay too long."

"Did it seem as though I wanted to spend the night?" Queen Fire asked, annoyed. She shook her head, her signature red earrings clinking back and forth. "I have a home to get to as well."

After what seemed like forever, they had made a dent in the amount of books on the shelves, but there were still hundreds of books left.

"I probably need to go see if my parents are home," Bella said. "I'll sneak back in. Do you want anything?"

"Water, please."

"Okay, be right back." Bella eased the bookcase to the side, opening it just enough for her to get through, then slid it back.

The great room was quiet and the kitchen still empty. Whew. Not having to sidestep Dad or—

"Mom, hi!" Bella said.

"Whoa, that was close," her mother said, smiling. "Careful, Bells. I'm old, and you can't plow into us old folk."

"Sorry!" The princess froze, unsure of what to do. *Act normal. Sit on the couch. Turn on the TV.* But what if Mom wanted to talk more? *Put on something that she hates. But—*

"What time is company coming?"

Bella tried not to react, but a streak of panic ran through her. Her ears started to feel warm, and she knew she was blushing—something she always did when she tried to lie.

"Bella, come on." Queen Katherine reached out and touched her elbow. "I was just teasing. Are you sure everything is okay?"

"Completely sure," Bella said. "I'm just really

thirsty." Bella dashed to the kitchen and got bottled waters from the fridge.

She twisted the cap off one of the bottles and started drinking the water quickly. She skirted around her mom and sat on the couch. She flicked on the TV.

"I'll be on the back patio if you need me," Queen Katherine said.

Bella smiled and nodded.

After the back door shut, she counted to twenty before she leaped off the couch and ran to the bookcase.

"I'm so sorry," Bella said. "Here's your—"

The vault was empty, and all of the books had been returned to the shelves. Queen Fire had clearly found the crystal and gone home. The princess's debt to Queen Fire was paid. But that didn't mean Bella wanted the queen or king to know that she'd been in the vault and start asking questions.

One book near the end was upside down. Bella pulled it out and flipped the book over. STABLES was scratched into the back.

"Ugh," Bella said. She stamped her foot, not caring that she wasn't five. "I just want this to be over." Bella groaned again and rolled her eyes as she put the book back right side up.

She turned and smacked directly into Queen Katherine, with Ivy trailing close behind. Ivy, looking pale, mouthed, "I'm sorry" to her best friend.

Bella felt her heart drop to her toes.

10

Reunited . . . but Are They United?

Queen Katherine took off for the stables, and Bella had to work to keep up with her mom.

"Mom, wait. Can we talk first?" Bella pleaded.

The queen ignored her and made a beeline down the stable aisle.

"Where are you going?" Bella asked.

"To the exact spot where my sister and I used to almost live when we were your age," the queen said.

She stopped in front of Glimmer's stall and slid the door open.

"Katherine," Queen Fire said, locking eyes with her sister.

In one of her hands was the crystal. Queen Fire halted, quietly closing the stall door.

"Were you going back on your word?" Bella asked. "You obviously found the crystal in the vault and then you came *here*. Why?"

"I did find the crystal. My locator spell worked perfectly." The queen eyed Bella, her gaze settling on the "stables" book. "So you figured out how to find me," Queen Fire said. "But I also found the book that you had seen, Bella, with this note. I knew it wasn't some childish act of vandalism. The word "stables" was the only clue that I needed. It led me here."

Bella's eyes wandered from her mom to Queen Fire. Six guards flanked Bella and her mom. They had been so silent that Bella hadn't even heard them approach. Bella looked over her shoulder, and three more guards stood silent and still behind Queen Fire. Bella locked eyes with Glimmer. As much as the unicorn disliked Queen Fire, she was standing still and on her best behavior.

"Tell me the truth, Fawn," Queen Katherine said. "Did you come here for the crystal or for something else?"

The guards tensed, ready to pounce if Queen Fire said the wrong thing. Whatever "wrong" was.

"The crystal," Queen Fire said. "I came for the photographs it holds, Katherine. Of us. Of our childhood."

Bella shook her head, sure she'd heard wrong. She hadn't allowed herself to think much about what the crystal did. That somehow made it easier to steal from the castle and give to Queen Fire.

"Guards, I have the situation under control. You're free to go." Queen Katherine leaned down to face Bella. "As for you, I can tell you that we are going to have a very, *very* long talk about all of this when your father gets home."

"I know." Bella cast her eyes down. "I'm sorry."

She was ready for Queen Katherine to tell her to go to her room and not expect to ride Glimmer for weeks. Months.

Queen Katherine let out a big breath. "I know you are," she said. "Why don't you take Glimmer out for a walk and let me talk to my . . . sister. We clearly have a lot to discuss." Bella looked from her mom to Queen Fire. The sisters exchanged small smiles.

"Come on, Glimmer," Bella said. Glimmer sidestepped Queen Fire and trotted after Bella as she left the stables. Bella felt lighter than she had in a week. She knew that she was still in big trouble for lying to her parents. As she looked back at her mom and aunt, she tried to imagine how close they used to be and hoped this might help them speak again. Maybe one day they would all end up at Queen Fire's castle, enjoying that Dark Forest cake as one big family.

But for now, the one thing Bella knew for sure? Glimmer was safe and all hers.

Acknowledgments

Many, many thanks to my team at Simon & Schuster who made *The Hidden Treasure*, well, magic! Hugs to Mara Anastas, Alyson Heller, Fiona Simpson, Jessica Handelman, and everyone from sales to design who had a hand in crafting this book.

Victoria Ying, your illustrations brought Bella, Glimmer, and their friends to life—thank you!

Endless appreciation to my friends, Cali Family, and the amaze Agent Jenn.

Thank-yous to the teachers, librarians, booksellers, and reviewers everywhere!

Finally, to my readers—you are the true princesses and princes!